Harriet Clare &

Secret Notebook #2

colour me

yum!e!

Harriet Clare

PINKIE SWEAR!

BOOOO!!!

Secret Notebook #2

Indie and I are there. Where are you?
Quick! Put yourself in the photo.

Harriet and _Lily-mae_
BFFs 4EVER!

My **NEW** Best Friends!

Sunday April 5th

1:30 pm

I am so sleepy! Like, big, eye-shutting,

scrunched-up-face and non-stop-yawning sleepy!

And don't say it! I know already. I KNOW!

It's only the start of the afternoon, right?

But to me it feels like

the middle of the night.

I'm so tired that my

face looks like Puglet's!

Bahaha! ZZZZ...

1

And do you know why I'm SOOOOOO tired?

I finally had my sleepover last night

with Indie, Ella and Ruby. YAY!

The four of us, all together! How cool is

that?! And having three friends for

just an ordinary sleepover at my house is a lot!

Well, a not-so-ordinary sleepover because it was

MEGA-EXCELLENT! Everyone said so.

Not just me. Oh, okay, okay. I did say it was

mega-excellent. They said it was the best! BUT

it really, seriously was MEGA-ExCELLENT!

HEY, if I tell you a secret about Ella and Ruby, do you **pinkie swear** to keep it a secret? **PROMISE?**

Okay, the secret is that I didn't like Ella and Ruby for a while. I thought they were yucky.

OOOH! AAAGH! ELLA AND RUBY! PUKE! I used to sing.

But the thing is, I only didn't like them because my absolute **BEST** friend, Indie, hung out with them when she didn't like me.

I was heaps sad!

It was after I (accidentally, truly didn't mean to,

cross my heart and hope to die) cut a hole in

Indie's uniform. AAAAGH! I know! I know!

SHHHHH! It was soooooo bad and I want

to forget all about it! Like REALLY, TRULY

FORGET.

Anyway, how dumb was that?

I didn't like Ella and Ruby and

thought they were mean

and nasty JUST

BECAUSE Indie played with

them when she didn't like me.

I know it was silly and wrong. I mean, I didn't even know them really, but I couldn't help it!

I couldn't stop myself <u>NOT</u> liking **THEM** because Indie was playing with them and <u>NOT</u> with **ME**.

SOB!

At least I only wrote what I thought about them in my secret notebook. I NEVER, EVER said it out loud.

PROMISE!

I was all alone! WAH!

And I didn't say bad things about them to anyone ... Well, I did tell **Puglet**, but she knows how to keep a secret and she doesn't even have to **Pinkie swear** on it!

I won't tell anyone!

Anyway, now that Indie and I are **besties** again, I've become really good friends with Ella and Ruby, too. And you know what? They are **SOOOOO** cool and not even a teeny-weeny bit yucky! We all hang out together now and I **LOVE, LOVE, LOVE** it!

Here's a picture I drew of Ella and Ruby
in their sleepover skirts, shorts and shirts.

LOVE LOVE LOVE it!

cool

Sometimes
Ruby gets
called Ruby-Lou.
Mostly by
her mum.

Gabriella is Ella's
real name, but
she likes to be
called Ella.

They've got
skirts, too!
Soooo jealous.

Draw two of your friends for me.
Finish off my border, too! I ❤ doing borders!

Friends

8

We all have the same style of shorts and t-shirts!
We LOVE pom-pom shorts but I'm a teensy
bit jealous of Ella's. Well ... um ... actually, a lot
jealous of them. They're so SPARKLY and pretty!

I asked if she wanted to swap and she
just laughed and said NO WAY! So I said
she had to swap with me or I'd put a spell on her.

BAHAHAHA!

HAHAHA...!

And she just laughed
even more! HAHAHA!

Me casting
my spell!

Ella has **THE BEST** laugh. It makes us all roll around on the floor laughing even when we don't know what's funny!

But back to pom-pom shorts and tops now. I got my shorts and top with Indie when we went shopping with our mums.

I took ages and ages to choose which ones I wanted. Indie knew which ones she wanted straight away.

Indie is like that. She always knows what she likes and she **never** changes her mind afterwards. I wish I was like

Indie's a star!

that. I always think I know, and then I see what **someone else** has chosen, and sometimes I wish

I'd picked what they picked. Not always ... just sometimes.

Oh, maybe, a bit more than just sometimes. **BLEH!**

Do you ever do that? Please say yes! It's okay to be like that, isn't it?

Anyway, this time I ended up going scary because I LOVE scary.

BOO!

HAHAHA!

I thought these PJs were totally awesome ... until I saw Ella's. Oh well. Got it wrong, again!

What would you pick? Tell me! Create your most favourite pattern in the whole wide world. I bet I'll want your shorts and top!

Show me your FAVOURITE shorts and top.

HURRY!

meow   mean

I'm dying to
see them!

Meow

I fell asleep! In the middle of the afternoon!
 who does that? Sorry, sorry, sorry.

I was just so tired. zzz... zzz... zzz...

NOW! I need to write about my **MOST**

EXCELLENT sleepover party that wasn't

really a party but I still planned

everything just like it was a

party because it was

kinda, sorta my very late

Birthday party

14

My birthday was at the end of February.

I KNOW! I KNOW! It's April already and

who celebrates their birthday nearly six weeks

late? ME! THAT'S WHO!

I'll tell you why in a minute but first I think

I should play five questions. I mean, I haven't

even told you my actual birthday or anything.

Do you know how to play? It's easy. We both have

to answer the same five questions. I go first

and you go after me.

So, are you ready to play?

15

Harriet Clare's Favourite Five

QUESTION 1: Do you have a nickname?

ME: Well, yeah! But only really special people like my mum and dad and besties know.

It's Clare Bear.

It's a nickname I've had since I was an itty bitty baby!

Me Bear!

YOU:

_____

_____

_____

_____

_____

QUESTION 2: How old are you and when were you born?

ME: I'm 8 years, 5 weeks and 1 day old.

I was born on February 29th.

I only get two candles. THAT SUCKS!

This year was a **leap year** so I really got to have a birthday! When it isn't a leap year there's no February 29th! How weird is that?! It's a bit **special and Weird** at the same time!

YOU: _____

_____

_____

_____

_____

QUESTION 3: What's your favourite playground game?

ME: Harrietball! BAHAHA!

It's a game I made up that's kinda like handball.

It's for four players. We play with our lucky

Harriet balls!

rubber **glitter** balls.

Mine's blue. I love bouncing

it and watching the glitter

float around inside it.

YOU:

_____

_____

_____

_____

QUESTION 4: Do you like boys?

ME: Sometimes! Mostly, boys are YUCK and GROSS but some are COOL!

Like, Ella's twin brother, Mannie. *Mannie rocks!*

He's SUPER-duper-cool but that's different because he's Ella's twin brother. DUH!

My brother is pretty cool, too. But only sometimes! The rest of the time he is SOOOOO annoying!

YOU: _____

_____

_____

_____

QUESTION 5: What's the biggest thing you've gotten into trouble for?

ME: Umm ... welllll ...

I'm scared that if I

write about it, you'll

think I'm like really

naughty.

I'm not! Honest and

I would even pinkie swear

I'm an angel!
Truly!

that I'm not! It's just that sometimes things ...

oh, you know! They don't always

turn out the way you think ...

Okay, here's one thing and not the biggest thing.

Not the smallest thing either! Just one thing.

Well, April Fools' Day was last Wednesday and I

played the **BEST PRANK EVER** on my brother.

You remember

Ethan Clare, right?

My very annoying,

smelly

brother I call EClare?

Well, I got him really

good! Maybe too good.

I filled a bucket with water and just a few drops of red food colouring. It made the

water go a really pretty pink!

Then I got up super early and

used the stepladder to climb up and balance the

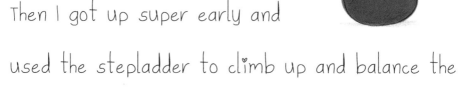

Red food colouring

bucket on the top of EClare's bedroom door.

When he opened the door the bucket fell on him.

BAHAHAHA!

And I was right there ready to take a photo on my mobile phone.

SOOOO GOOD!

The **trouble** was he should have come through the door in his pyjamas. But he didn't. He was all dressed for school in his white shirt and shorts. OH NOOOO! I had forgotten he had band practice before school.

NOOOO!

AAARGH! His shirt had pretty pink wet patches all over it and so did the carpet in his doorway. OOOPS!

But it was so funny that I could hardly breathe for laughing! I mean, you should have seen how funny his face was! But EClare didn't laugh **AT ALL**.

He was **5000** mad I thought he was going to pop his freckles.

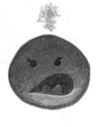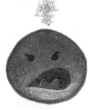

And what was worse was that Mum didn't laugh either when she saw what I'd done.

She went nuts! And I mean like, **hopping-mad nuts!** **AND** she didn't call me Clare Bear, THAT'S FOR SURE!

Uh oh! It was bad!

AND even WORSE still was that I thought that food colouring washed out. I really did! But it doesn't seem to wash out much at all! EEEEK! Then, because Mum and Dad hadn't done

any washing on the weekend, EClare had to go to school like that! SOOO BAD!

EClare hasn't talked to me ALL WEEK and I got into SO MUCH TROUBLE.

I have to tidy up my bedroom now. I promised Mum I would. I'll write all about the sleepover party after.

Still Sunday April 5th but My New Chapter!

7:00 pm

YEP! I'm already in bed. I'm SOOOOOOO

tired that I'm not even writing this from my

secret hiding place. (YAWN!)

I love my bed! It has heaps and heaps

of stuffed animals on it. There are so many toy

pugs that sometimes I can't find Puglet when she

curls up and sleeps on it. BAHAHAHA!

♥ Pugs!

Can you find Puglet? Do you like my new quilt?
I think it's cool!

zzzz...

I got no sleep
last night!

SOOOO, now I'll explain why I didn't have a **Birthday party** when it was my birthday. It was because ...

deep breath ... don't cry ...

just tell, **Harriet Clare!**

My grandma died. There. I told.

Uh-oh ... SNIFF... hiccup.

OH, NO! I'm crying really, really **big** now.

tissues

Crying SOOOOO big that I'm making those

weird gulping noises that make you want to

burst out laughing but you're too busy crying

really, really big! And now

Puglet is licking my face

like crazy!

If I don't stop crying,

she will start to cry, too.

Puddle
of tears

She's SO cute. She hates it

when I'm upset and covers

her eyes with her paws!

PLEASE STOP!

STOP!

WAAAA!

The thing is, we knew Grandma was dying. Uh-oh ...

GULP, SNORT, HICCUP... Sorry for blubbing

but I miss her SO much. So, I decided to wait

to have a party.

Then, by the time I felt like doing something, I didn't

feel like having a party any more. So, I just had a

small bestie sleepover and I'm SO glad I did.

Sometimes I miss Grandma SOOOO much it hurts. Before she died, she gave me an engraved "guardian angel" bracelet. I ALWAYS

wore it because Grandma said that when I wore it, she would always be close to me.

Don't you just love it?

Do you have any bracelets or bangles that you ABSOLUTELY love?

Grandma also gave me these plants on my windowsill. She said that after she died she would send me a sign and that the **sign** would be that these plants would flower. Grandma was always saying **funny stuff** HAHAHA... like that and I didn't really get what she meant but every day I wish the plants would **flower** and every day there's no flowers. **SOB! SOB! SOB!**  ← tear

Grandma lived with us, and when I had friends staying over she LOVED feeding us her famous spaghetti and meatball cupcakes, and doing our hair. So, of course we had a hair contest and ate spaghetti cupcakes at my sleepover! I think my cupcakes turned out almost as well as Grandma's! YUM!

All that stringy cheese, spaghetti and Grandma's secret-sauce recipe!

I love those cupcakes.

Real spaghetti and meatballs in cupcake cases!

Uh-oh! Think I'm going to be in trouble now!

Yum!

Yum!

37

When it came to our hair contest,

Mum worked the hair straightener

and curling tongs for us instead of Grandma. I had

baskets of ribbons, clips, hair chalk and all sorts

of awesome hair decorations from

the bargain store for us to use.

I did Ella's hair.

Ella did Indie's.

Indie did Ruby's

and Ruby did mine.

And then we voted on the hairstyles!

love

Tell me how you'd vote. What do you think of our mad new styles? Do you *like* our hairdos?

YOUR TURN! Do your best and
don't you DARE give me *frizzy hair!*

41

After the hair contest, we played ... **OH. WAIT!**

Before I tell you that, I have to tell you how **WE**

voted in the **hair contest**. We voted equal first

for all four of us **HA-HA!** We had soooo much fun.

Anyway, after that, of course we had to play

TRUTH or **DARE** while we munched away

on **WICKED** snacks!

I actually made my own game especially for the sleepover. Can you believe it? GO ME! And I had some serious fun doing it! I came up with all the TRUTH questions **AND** all the DARES. I wrote them out on the special **Harriet Clare**

TRUTH or **DARE** cards that I made myself, as well!

Check out the board with the spinner! DO YOU LOVE IT? Would you be brave enough to play it?

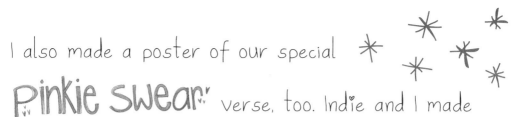

I also made a poster of our special

Pinkie swear
verse, too. Indie and I made

it up. Well, we found the first two lines on the

Internet and we made the rest up. **TRUE!**

We say it for **ALL** our secrets and we **NEVER.**

EVER. EVER.

break a pinkie

swear. **EVER!**

'N.E.V.E.R.

BFFs 4 EVER!

I will not bend,
I will not break,
This pinky swear
I now do make.
I'll never tell
the secrets told,
This pinky swear
will always hold.

So, the four of us linked pinkie fingers and said the **verse** together before we started playing truth or dare. Because EVERYONE knows that you must NEVER EVER, no matter what, tell the truths shared.

Boy, there were some really OMG truths told! I got all dares. SO WEIRD! I didn't spin one single truth.

My dares are nuts! Bahahaha!!!

I got a dare to go to the toilet and leave the door open! BAHAHAHA! Why did I write a dare like that? OMG! I AM CRAZY!

I'm super tired now and really have to go to sleep. I CAN'T WAIT to get to school tomorrow and talk about all the fun things we did at the sleepover and how good it was! Tomorrow will be THE BIGGEST,

Time for bed Harriet Clare!

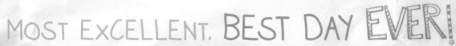

MOST EXCELLENT, BEST DAY EVER!

Monday April 6th

4:30 pm

OMG! What a **MASSIVE NIGHTMARE DAY!**

I wish I'd never gotten out of bed! REALLY!

I cannot believe what happened today.

No bracelet

It all started when I went to put on

Grandma's guardian angel bracelet and it

was gone! NOOOO! I turned my room

upside down and wanted

to stay home and keep looking for

it but Mum made me go to school.

49

I got there late and didn't get to play before school or talk to anyone. I REALLY wanted to talk to Ruby because the last time I saw my bracelet was when we were telling each other ghost stories

Bracelet

in bed. She was wearing it then and I thought that maybe she'd forgotten to take it off.

SOOOO, I passed her this note in class but I got CAUGHT! BOOOOOO! ☹

I'm keeping it in here as EVIDENCE! I mean, there's nothing bad in that note, is there? BUT OMG! wait till I tell you what happened next.

Hey Ruby,

Did you take my

guardian angel bracelet

home by mistake? It's just

that I can't find it and

you were wearing it last.

Your friend, HC.

First, Miss Henrietta kept me back at morning tea to talk about **my behaviour** in class! UUUGH! Then, by the time I made it to the handball courts, Ella, Ruby and Indie were already playing Harrietball with Gracie and her **AMAZING** new glitter ball.

Every time Gracie's ball hit the ground it **CHANGED COLOUR** and ·Sparkly·lights· went off inside it! I could not **STOP** staring at it.

WANT!   WANT!   WANT!   WANT!

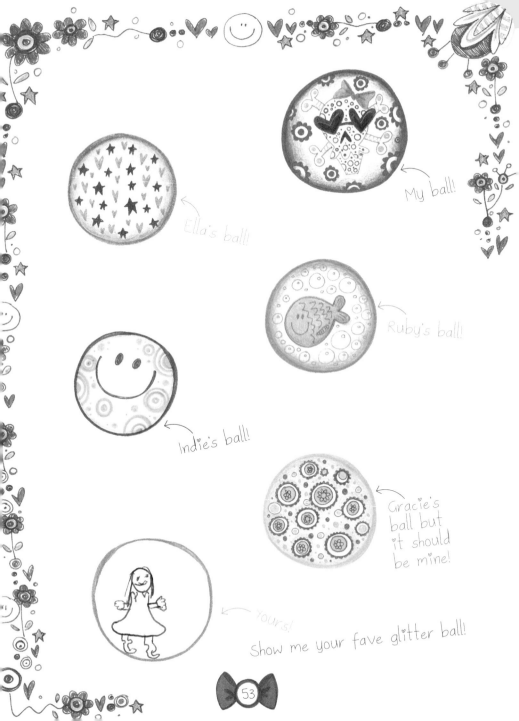

Ella's ball!

My ball!

Ruby's ball!

Indie's ball!

Gracie's ball but it should be mine!

Yours!

Show me your fave glitter ball!

Anyway, while I was waiting for the game to end I asked Ruby about the note and my bracelet. She got all **crazy mad** and **grumpy** and started shouting about how she didn't steal my dumb bracelet and what kind of friend would think something like that?!?

WHAT?!! I NEVER SAID SHE STOLE IT. AAAAAGH!

OH NO!

Did I write something dumb in my note? What would you have written? Tell me, pretty please!

TO Ruby

do you Know yesterday at the sleep over did you accidently take my my braclet

from lily-mae

THEN, in the middle of Ruby shouting at me. Paris and Lola skipped around Ella singing:

Ella and Jack, sitting in a tree, K.I.S.S.I.N.G

And that's when the game stopped and we all stood absolutely still, mouths gaping.

Paris and Lola kept on singing.

Ella was asked in truth or dare if she had a crush on a boy and she'd told us that she thought Jack was pretty cool.

← This is Jack.

56

Ella's cheeks went all red and not from playing! I felt really sorry for her. Then, after Paris and Lola skipped away, Ella threw her hands up and asked who broke the pinkie swear from the sleepover and blabbed to Paris and Lola.

Someone blabbed!

Not me!

YIKES

No way! As if!

Never!

MAJOR AWFUL!

who would have

broken the

pinkie swear?

And it didn't stop there! At lunch, I sat next to Ruby. I wanted to **explain** that I didn't think she stole my bracelet but before I could say anything she got up and moved to the other side of Indie!

OOOUUCH!

Ella tried to act like it didn't happen and asked where I'd gotten my lunchbox. In that moment I thought Ella Chen was one of the most **awesome** girls on the **planet!**

Ella Rocks!

Indie gave me a lunchbox for my **Birthday**. It came with special pens so you can decorate it any way you like.

I've done a bit.

You do the rest!

Then, two boys came over and started teasing Indie about being SCARED of the deep end at swimming school. OMG! I thought I was going to be sick. Another broken truth or dare PINKIE SWEAR!

I don't want to jump!

I looked at Ella and she glared back at me. I said that it wasn't me who blabbed. Then I turned to Indie to see if she was okay.

But you know what Indie did? She stood up, closed her eyes and took a deep breath. Then she looked straight at those boys and said that at least she knew what she was afraid of and how to **face her fears.** She told them that she'd already talked to her swimming coach and that her coach was going to give her a private lesson in the deep end and how cool was that?!

I do want to jump!

And then she said that she didn't care who knew

and that facing your fears was way better than

teasing people to make yourself feel big!

AND THEN ... she just sat down again.

 Those boys didn't know what to

do so they just walked away.

And that is why I LOVE HER.

Well, that is just one of the

hundreds and thousands

of reasons why I love her TO

BITS and am so glad that she's my friend.

Indie Charlton is a legend!

BUT THEN, just when I thought

things couldn't get any worse, they got

mega-mega-MASSIVELY WORSE!

That afternoon, during reading group, just about

the whole class seemed to know that Ruby had

admitted to cheating to win a game.

They were all whispering that she was a cheat!

NOOOOO!

Ruby CHEATS!

Who'd play with HER?!

She's a BIG cheat.

I know! BOO on her!

IT WAS HORRIBLE. xx

But what happened when the bell rang to go home was EVEN MORE HORRIBLE STILL.

UUUGH!

Ella and Ruby being mean.

As we were packing up our bags, Ella and Ruby said that obviously I was the one who broke the pinkie swear and **told** everyone's secrets because I was the only one out of the four of us who hadn't had any secrets spread about them!

But I hadn't gotten any truth cards in the game! I'd only gotten **dares!**.

Me trying not to sob. WAAAAAH!

OMG!

I could feel Ella, Ruby and Indie's eyes on me and I just stared at my feet. I wish I was more like Indie. <u>I WISH</u> I had said everything I wanted to say. But I couldn't. I knew I was starting to cry and I didn't want Ella and Ruby to see that.

So, I ran to my Mum's car with Indie running

after me. Right before I got in the car, Indie

grabbed me and said that she didn't believe

FOR ONE SECOND that it was me

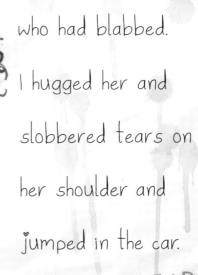

who had blabbed.

I hugged her and

slobbered tears on

her shoulder and

jumped in the car.

SOB. SNIFF. SOB. SOB.

HICCUP.

tear

When I woke up this morning,

my **he♥art** felt like this. ⇨

Right now, my **he♥art**

feels like this. ⇨

What should have

been the best day

ended up being the

worst day

ever!

NOOOO!

STILL the BIGGEST, MOST HORRIBLE, WORST DAY EVER!

Monday April 6th

8:00 pm

It's really late, I know! But Mum and I had a big long talk after "jazz ballet" class and then she said I could still write in my notebook if I wanted to because she thought it might make me feel better.

I don't feel better though.

Not yet, anyway ...

And so far all I've done is doodle!

Do you want to do some? GO ON!

Doodling makes everyone feel better.

It always works for me!

I feel a bit better now and not so sad.

So, now I'll tell you what Mum said.

I told her

everything!

Even the truth-

or-dare bits and

she didn't even blink.

I did though! I felt a bit WEIRD!

I can't believe I told Mum all those things!

Mum said she could see how Ella and Ruby might

have decided it was me that blabbed

even though she knew I hadn't.

Mum also said that she didn't think anyone took my bracelet and that it would turn up eventually. Then she said that she had an idea and that she needed to go and make a few phone calls to organise a trip to Yoghurt YOUniverse after school tomorrow. Then she kissed me goodnight and left. VERY WEIRD!

Yoghurt YOUniverse ROCKS
and so does my mum!

Tuesday April 7th

6:00 pm

OMG! My stomach! I had to lie down on the floor.
I am **so full** from yoghurt parfait! And Puglet

keeps climbing on top of me and curling up on

my **way-too-full** stomach!

She's going to make me throw up!

Yoghurt YOUniverse **rocks!**

But my mum rocks even more! She's like

the world's best problem-solver and the

MOST EXCELLENT MUM ever!

Everything is all sorted and you won't  **BELIEVE** who broke the pinkie swear!

But first I have to show you the yoghurt parfait I made!  **YUMMO!** There are so many different flavoured yoghurts and AWESOME add-ons to choose from that it's almost impossible to decide what to pick! But this time I got it just right!

And I didn't want what everyone else chose for once. **YIPPEE!**

GO ME!
Parfait Queen!

MY PARFAIT

Chocolate sprinkles!

This is my yoghurt YOUniverse parfait.

Banana and nuts

Chocolate chip frozen yoghurt. YUM!

Strawberry jelly... mmmmmm...

YUMYUMYUM!

74

What's your parfait glass filled with?

Don't forget to *decorate* the top of it!

75

Okay, SO today Mum organised to pick up Indie, Ella, Ruby, EClare and me from school. Then she took us all to **Yoghurt YOUniverse** in her van ... OBVIOUSLY!

Then, she said that EClare had something to say to us. Well, my mouth dropped open and I sat there waiting for him to speak.

After what felt like the **longest time** *tic tic tic tic tic tic tic tic tic tic* ever, EClare finally began talking.

HE SAID:

1. I was **REALLY, REALLY** *mad* with Harriet for the prank she played on me on April Fools' Day and I decided to get her back.

2. At the sleepover, I hid my mobile phone in Harriet's room and I turned the **recorder app ON**.

EClare's mobile phone →

3. On Sunday, I snuck in and got my mobile phone back. The battery was dead but I charged it and listened to you guys playing **truth** or **dare** and you can figure out the rest.

I can't breathe! AAAAARGH!

Then, Mum said that he had something else to tell but I had already stopped breathing! **I SWEAR** I had! I didn't think I could take any more! Mum must have known because then she suggested that we all get changed so that our uniforms would stay clean for tomorrow.

When we came back, Mum told EClare

to finish what he had to say.

Then, EClare looked really embarrassed

and reached into his pocket. **OMG!**

He placed my guardian angel bracelet

on the table and said that he took it

because he knew how much I loved it

and he wanted to make me feel as

OMG!
He took
it?

EClare's
BUSTED!

miserable as he did

when he had to go to school

in a shirt stained with

pink patches.

79

No one spoke. SERIOUSLY. And I still wasn't breathing. I was sure of it!

We all must have looked SO SILLY sitting there with our mouths hanging open. Had Grandma been there, she would have asked us if we were catching flies and told us to close our mouths. BAHAHAHA! I LOVE Grandma's sayings!

And then, if all of that wasn't enough. Mum said

that she thought that someone needed to say they

were **SOrry**.

AND SHE LOOKED
AT ME! ME???!!!!!

I looked to my friends for **help** but they just

sat there with their mouths still hanging open.

What's going on?
Somebody help me!

Then, I looked at EClare and

suddenly it hit me that he

had done all these awful things

because of a silly **PRANK**

that I had played on him.

As I sat there with my mouth still open and my brain racing, I thought about how much I'd hated this last week with EClare not talking to me. How much I had missed playing games with him, watching TV together and just goofing around.

And just as I was about to say sorry, EClare began to talk again.

EClare said that even though he was mad at me, getting back at me the way he had was **wrong** and he felt bad about it.

I told him that I thought food colouring washed out and that he was **meant** to be in his pyjamas when it fell on him, **NOT** his school clothes. I told him that I was **really sorry** about his pink shirt.

He said that he was actually a teensy-weensy bit impressed

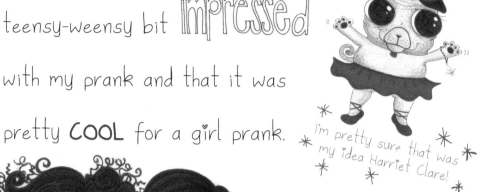

with my prank and that it was pretty **COOL** for a girl prank.

I'm pretty sure that was my idea Harriet Clare!

And I grinned the

biggest grin

since Saturday night.

Then suddenly, Ruby spoke up and said that she always takes things the wrong way and she doesn't know why, **but she does!**

why does Ruby do that? Who knows!

I said that I never thought she **stole** my

bracelet and she said that she **knew** that.

Mum's mega coffee!

And Mum said that she thought

she'd earned a really **big** cup

of coffee and went to order one.

Then, we all burst out laughing and we didn't even

know why! **we just did.**

HA!

HAHAHA

HA

HA

HA

HA

HA

HA

HA

We laughed so hard we almost cried and then Indie grabbed the box of markers that always sit on the tables at Yoghurt YOUniverse.

She took out a **black** marker and divided the paper tablecloth into six equal rectangles. She demanded a <u>doodle draw-off</u> and said that no one was allowed to get a parfait until a doodle-draw WINNER was declared.

And the beyond-the-best-of-the-best thing **ever**

was that when we got home Mum said there was

a **SURPRISE** for me in my room.

Look at what it was!

A SIGN FROM GRANDMA!

WOOOHOOO

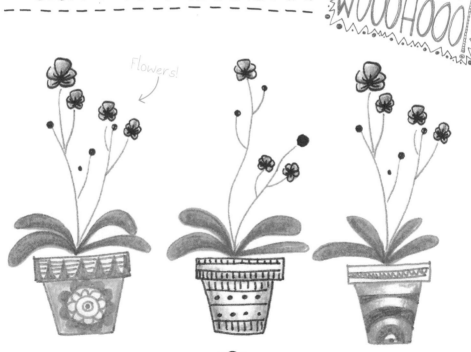

Flowers!

YAY!

Dance Concert Week is FINALLY HERE!

Sunday May 17th

7:30 pm

YEP! It's our dance concert on Friday night and Indie and I are SO excited! OH. MY. GOSH.

YAHOOOOO!

And the best thing ever is that Indie's mum is bringing our friends Ella and Ruby to the concert to watch us dance! They'll all be sitting with Mum, Dad and my brother, the BIG ECLARE, in the front row. COOOOL CUPCAKES with sprinkles on top!

HEY! I'm on the internet!
GO ME! How cool is that?!
www.harrietclare.com.au

Have you read my first notebook?

Published by Hinkler Books Pty Ltd
45–55 Fairchild Street
Heatherton Victoria 3202 Australia
www.hinkler.com.au

© Hinkler Books Pty Ltd 2015

hinkler

ISBN: 978 1 4889 2681 5

Printed and bound in China